HUGO SPROUTS

AND the STRANGE CASE of the BEANS

by JOHN LOREN

I bet you've heard stories, or read the adventures
of wily young whiz kids, or expert inventors. . . .

Well, this one's a **whopper**! You see, there's no doubt,
the cleverest ever was:

Why, nothing could rival his powerful passion
to think up and tinker astounding contraptions!

THE SELF-TIMING TOAST-BOT!

THE FLAPJACK-O-MATIC!

THE BUBBLEGUM JETPACK!

REMOTE-CONTROL HADDOCK!

But despite all the theorems and figures he'd cracked,
one problem still lingered . . . a **big** one, in fact.

See, with seven assorted Sprouts sisters and brothers,
young Hugo was smaller than all of the others.

The older Sprouts kids, who were taller and thicker,
always got picked to play kickball much quicker.

"He's simply too shrimpy!" the pickers would snicker.
"This kid and his pup are just pitiful kickers!"

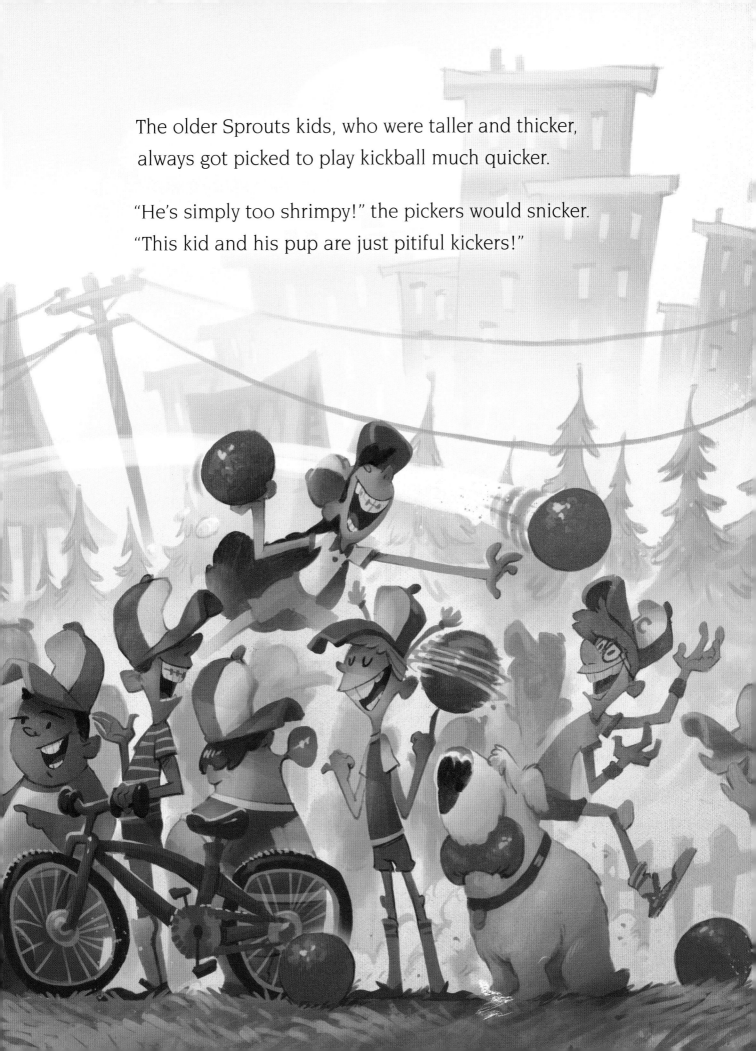

Trudging back home
with his barely kicked ball,
sighed Hugo,
"I'm tired of being too small!"

"Too young for the movies!
Too short for the rides!"

"My bedtime is early!
My cones are kid-size!"

"Things would be better,"
he wondered aloud,
"if I could be bigger, I figure,
but **how**?"

"Try THIS!" said his pop, with his mustache aquiver.
"Eat up your lima beans, choke down some liver!"

"Just gulp these garbanzos, and slurp some soy slop!
And THAT'S how you grow big and strong like your pop!"

They dripped with gross gravy that made Hugo flinch,
but he gulped down a bean...

and grew not one inch.

"That does it!" he grumbled. "These beans are too slow.
Let's fix up a quicker solution to grow!
Off to the lab now, Ulysses, and hurry!"

(Ulysses said nothing but looked a bit worried.)

Plop! went the beans in a shimmering stew,
and they cooked up a cauldron of gooey green brew!
They toiled and troubled 'til two without stoppin'. . . .

At last! They had boiled the perfect concoction!
"Eureka!" cried Hugo, and threw back his head.
He poured down some potion, and skipped off to bed.

The very next day, when they gathered for chow,
the Sprouts' little kitchen seemed smaller somehow. . . .

"How splendid!" said Hugo. "You know what this means?
My potion's more potent than boring ol' beans!
Come on, Ulysses! This growing thing's easy!"

(Ulysses stayed quiet but looked a bit queasy.)

He rode the Puke-Looper and Spinny-Go-Twist.

He conquered the kickball game, fifty to six.

The kids were defiant. "No way—that's unfair!
You're pretty much giant—we hadn't a prayer!"

"hey, wait!" Hugo quipped.

"pretty much
just won't do!"

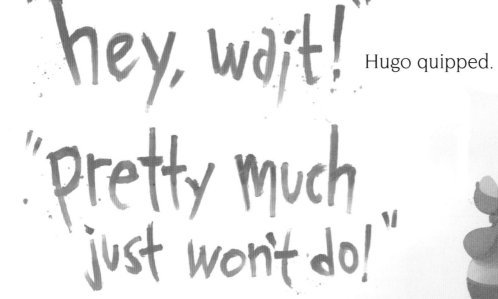

And he sipped up a drip of his potion . . .

and **grew!**

"Much better." He laughed as he gobbled up sweets.

Then caught the new movie (in sixty-two seats!)
The usher was flustered.
"Get down, you big goof!
You're nearly so huge, you could bust through the roof!"

"Nearly?" sneered Hugo.

"Why, that just won't do!"

And he swallowed a slurp of his potion . . .

and **grew!**

The mayor was deep in a tubful of bubbles
when news was delivered by phone of the trouble.

THE ORCHESTRA'S FLAT!

"Great Scott!" cried the mayor. "Gadzooks and good gravy!
Send word to the army and get me the navy!"

"I tell you, it's urgent, come pronto!" She gulped.
"A monster is stomping our city to pulp!"

"Hey, you there," she hollered. "Enough with this caper!
You're almost as tall as the tallest skyscraper!"

"ALMOST!?"

roared Hugo.

"that Simply Won't do!"

And he lifted the last drop of potion and—

"STOP!"

Ulysses, perched high on a swaying Sprouts tower,
had piped up at last, and, with all his small power,
he cried through the clouds, with a face sad and somber:
"Please stop! That's enough! We can take it no longer!"

"BAH!"

Hugo boomed,
and his gruesome teeth glistened.

"but now i'M the Biggest, So Why should i Listen?"

"Because," barked Ulysses, "it's you most of all
who knows what it's like being stepped on and small!
Today, you're the tallest, that much may be true,
but yesterday **you** were the one in our shoes."

"So Hugo, despite your new
height and your heft,
you've proved you've got plenty
of growing up left."

With that, he walked off in a huff and a snort.
And Hugo stood silent, without a retort.

And as he considered the things that he'd done,
he felt a bit smaller with each passing one.

So he set straight to work, with some help from the Sproutses,
and fixed all the dents in the shops and the houses.

He polished and prodded, he mended and dusted,
and buffed all the scuffs off the stuff he had busted.

At very long last, the whole town was restored,
and Hugo was finally kid-size once more.

That night, the whole city dropped in for a feast
of Pop's three-bean salad with liver and beets.

"Now, Hugo," Pop cautioned, "I really insist
you never repeat a fiasco like this."
"No, never!" swore Hugo. "I promise you, Dad,
I'm through with that potion, and beans aren't so bad."

"But where," pondered Pop,
"has that last drop got to?"

"That's funny," said Hugo.
"I haven't a clue. . . ."

For Andrew and Caroline.
Eat your beans.
Love, Pop

This book took a long time to grow big and strong. Humongous thanks to:
Lauren Appleton, Nicholas Kole, Jimmy Mullen, Brooks Sherman, Uncle Kurt, and the Lorens.
And to the HarperCollins team, Alison Klapthor, Corina Lupp, Jenny Ly, and Rich Thomas.

ISBN 978-0-06-294116-9

The illustrations and lettering were drawn by hand on a digital device.
Typography by Corina Lupp
21 22 23 24 25 RTLO 10 9 8 7 6 5 4 3 2 1
❖
First Edition